M E

Based on a story by V. Suteev

O W !

Retold and illustrated by Katya Arnold

Holiday House • New York

"MEOW!"

Puppy woke up.

Who said that? Who said meow?

There was no one in sight.

So he went back to sleep.

"MEOW!"

Puppy heard it again.

Who said that? Who said meow?

He looked under the couch.

He looked under the table.

He looked through the window.

But no one was there.

Then…

"MEOW!"

There it was again!

Who said that? Who said meow?

Puppy ran outside. He saw Rooster.

"Did you say meow?"

"Not me," said Rooster. "I say

COCK-A-DOODLE-DOO!"

Puppy looked around.

But no one else was there.

Then...

"MEOW!"

He heard it again.

Who said that? Who said meow?

Was it under the stairs?

He started to dig.

A little mouse jumped out.

"Did you say meow?"

"Meow here?? Meow near!!"

The little mouse rushed to hide.

"SQUEAK, SQUEAK!"

"MEOW!"

There it was again!

Who said that? Who said meow?

He came to a doghouse. A big dog jumped out.

"S...S...Sir, did you say meow?"

"Are you making fun of me, Puppy?

BOW-WOW-WOW!"

barked the dog.

Puppy ran and hid behind a fence.

Then...

"OW!!!" cried Puppy.

"BUZZ-ZZZ-ZZZ," buzzed the bee.

SPLASH!!

Puppy jumped into the pond.

He poked his head out of the water.

No one was there.

Then...

"MEOW!"

Who said that? Who said meow?

A fish swam nearby.

"Did you say meow?" asked Puppy.

The fish did not answer. It swished its tail
and swam into the deep water.

"Fish never talk," said Frog.

"It was you! You said meow!" shouted Puppy.

"Not me, silly puppy. Frogs just croak,

RIBBIT, RIBBIT!"

And Frog jumped into the pond.

Puppy wanted to go home.

His nose was all swollen. His fur was all wet.

When he got back to his room, he heard...

"MEOW!"

He looked up. Standing there,
on the windowsill, was a...

CAT!

"MEOW!" said the cat.

-YIP!"

"SH-SH-SS!"
hissed the cat.
She arched her back
and leaped
out of the window.

WOW!",

Puppy was happy.
He knew who said meow!
Now it was time for sleep.
But while he was dreaming,
he thought he heard something...

Author's Note

Vladimir Grigorievich Suteev was born in Russia in 1903. Often called the Russian Walt Disney, he was a remarkable artist, screenwriter, and movie director.

Suteev made his first animated movie in 1931 and directed more than 30 others during his long career. His sweet, funny, and action-packed movies are immensely popular among Russian children. But Suteev was not only a movie director—he also wrote and illustrated many children's books based on his films. Perhaps his multiple talents can be explained this way—he wrote stories with his left hand and drew pictures with his right!

In 1955 Suteev and an animator named V. Degterev collaborated on the film *Who Said Meow?* and later that year Suteev published a book based on it. The movie was enormously successful, and the book became a best-seller. Even today *Who Said Meow?* is often used as a kindergarten play in Russia.

I retold *Who Said Meow?* for this book. I hope that my version will be as popular as the original once was!

Copyright © 1998 by Katya Arnold
All Rights Reserved
Printed in the United States of America
First Edition

Library of Congress Cataloging-in-Publication Data
Arnold, Katya
Meow!/retold and illustrated by Katya Arnold; based on a story by
Vladimir Grigorievich Suteev.—1st ed.
p. cm.
Summary: While trying to find who keeps saying, "Meow," a dog
discovers the sounds made by other animals that he meets.
ISBN 0-8234-1361-6
[1. Dogs—Fiction. 2. Cats—Fiction. 3. Animal Sounds—Fiction.]
I. Suteev, V (Vladimir) II. Title.
PZ7.A7356Me 1998
[E]--dc21   97-31646 CIP AC

Design and typesetting: Yvette Lenhart